PASTRAMI MURDER

THE DARLING DELI SERIES, BOOK 1

PATTI BENNING

SUMMER PRESCOTT BOOKS PUBLISHING

CHAPTER ONE

Moira Darling breathed a sigh of relief as she turned the deadbolt on the front door of Darling's DELI-cious Delights. When she first opened the deli, she had thought that the winter season would be slow. Not many tourists would brave the cold and snowy western Michigan winters just to visit the small town of Maple Creek for a bowl of hot soup. What she hadn't counted on was how popular her warm, freshly made soups and sandwiches would be with the locals.

"Well, we survived another Friday evening," said Moira's daughter, Candice, as she plopped down into a chair with a yawn.

"Thanks for helping out on such short notice, sweetie," Moira said. "I know Danielle feels bad about having to take time off with so little warning. At least she'll be picking up your shift tomorrow, so you'll be able to have some fun this weekend."

"It doesn't matter anyway." Candice wrinkled her nose. "Chad canceled our date, and I haven't heard from him since. Apparently, I don't have a social life anymore." Moira felt a stab of pity as her daughter groaned and buried her face in her hands, blond hair cascading around her face.

Candice was twenty-years-old and had moved back to Maple Creek after getting her associate's degree in business at a small college two hours away. Moira couldn't help but worry about her daughter; besides the endless bad luck she seemed to have when it came to men, Candice also seemed to have no plans for her future. While Moira was more than happy to have her daughter around to help out at the deli, she hoped that Candice would find a dream of her own to follow sometime soon. Maple Creek was just too quiet for the vibrant twenty-year-old.

Moira ducked into the back of the deli to shrug her coat on and grab the white paper bag that held the sandwiches that would be their dinner. She took one last look around to make sure everything was put away that needed to be put away. The deli was like a second child to her, and she knew that its success was partially due to her careful tending. Of course, her brilliant employees and the delicious food also went a long way towards making Darling's DELIcious Delights a hit.

"Are we going, Mom?" Candice called from the front. "I'm starving."

"I'm coming, sweetheart." Moira gave the deli's kitchen one last glance and then shut off the lights.

CHAPTER TWO

The deli didn't open until the afternoon on week-
ends, but Moira always got to work at ten. While she
had faith that her employees could make great sandwiches, she preferred to do the soup of the day
herself when she could. Saturday's Soup of the Day
was one of her favorites, Leeky Soup. It was based on
an old potato and leek soup recipe that her grand-
mother had made on cold winter nights. Moira had
spiced the recipe up a bit, adding a pinch of chili
powder and just a dash of nutmeg. Since the temper-
ature would be far below freezing today, Moira
thought her customers might enjoy the extra heat.

She was just putting the finishing touches on the
huge pot of soup that she hoped would see them

through the day when she heard the deli's front door open. A moment later, Danielle peeked her face around the door to the kitchen.

"Do you ever do anything but work, Ms. D.?" she asked. "You know I'm perfectly capable of following a recipe myself."

"I know," Moira said, giving her employee a reassuring smile. Danielle had been working for her for almost six months, and Moira had yet to regret her decision to hire the young woman, even though Danielle had recently been fired from another restaurant. "I just don't want to get too wrapped up in the business side of running the deli and forget what this is all about—making good food and making people happy."

"Well, this place does both those things on a daily basis." Danielle came the rest of the way into the kitchen and made her way over to the sink to wash her hands. "We're one of the most popular places in town."

"Except for the Soup Shoppe." Moira made a face. "Ever since Henry franchised, and started producing those new TV ads, we've been losing customers." She saw Danielle's face tighten, and felt bad for mentioning Henry Devou—Danielle had worked for him before she began working for Moira, and Moira knew that Danielle still disliked her previous boss. "Though I can't complain," she added quickly. "We're still doing well enough... much better than I expected, in fact." When she had decided to open Darling's DELIcious Delights two years ago, she had only intended the business to be a hobby—something to keep her busy while Candice was in college. She had been shocked at the success that her soups and sandwiches had found in the small town.

"Hopefully..." Danielle began, but she was cut off by the arrival of Darrin, the assistant manager, the first employee that Moira had hired after the deli had become too much to handle on her own. He was a young man, a few years older than Candice, with shoulder-length black hair and a winning smile. Her customers loved him, and even better, he knew his way around the kitchen like a pro. As Darrin walked into the kitchen, he gave both of the women a quick grin and then inhaled deeply.

"Wow, something smells good," he said.

"It's Leeky Soup," Moira told him. "Both of you, grab a bowl. You can be my taste testers. See if you think I added too much chili powder to this batch."

CHAPTER THREE

Moira only stayed at the deli for a few hours. Once she made sure that her employees had everything running smoothly, she waved and left, deciding to do some grocery shopping before heading home and starting dinner for herself and Candice.

She was surprised to find the house empty when she got home. She put the grocery bags down in the kitchen and saw the quickly scrawled note on the fridge. *Out with Samantha. I'll be home later. XOXOXO*

Moira was glad that Candice had gotten over her boyfriend troubles so quickly, and was having fun with one of her friends, but couldn't help feeling slightly sorry for herself. As a divorced woman in her early forties, her own dating pool was quite small. Moira knew that she looked good for her age. She had a petite frame, light brown hair that hadn't really begun to go gray, and what her husband had described as mischievous green eyes... at least during the early years of their marriage. Even though she thought of herself as an attractive, intelligent go-getter, her dates always seemed to fizzle out before the end of the evening. In fact, she couldn't even remember the last time she had been on a date with a guy that she actually liked. *I really need to get out there more*, she thought. *As much as I love my job, I need more in my life than work.* Moira shook her head to clear her mind. She had always found self-pity very undesirable. Besides, she had a lot to live for; a wonderful daughter, a thriving business and... well, that was enough, wasn't it? With a sigh, she began putting away the groceries. She would make a nice dinner another night when Candice was home. For now, she could eat leftovers. In fact, leftovers and a TV marathon were starting to sound like a pretty good way to spend her Saturday evening.

Moira woke up to her cell phone ringing. She felt

around for it on her bedside table, slid her finger across the screen, and then brought the phone to her ear.

"Hello," she said, feeling groggy.

"Have you seen the news yet, Ms. D.?" Darrin's voice came over the phone.

"No... why? What time is it?" Moira sat up in bed, feeling disoriented. She glanced at the clock, and saw that it was shortly after ten. She had stayed up late the night before, eating leftovers, drinking wine, and watching reruns of her favorite show. She realized that she hadn't heard Candice come in at any point during the night. Suddenly worried, Moira slid out of bed and pulled her bathrobe on, keeping the phone pressed between her shoulder and her ear.

"Is something going on?"

"Henry Devou, you know, the guy that owns the Soup Shoppe... he's dead," Darrin told her.

"Oh, my goodness, what happened?" Moira asked. She couldn't help feeling relieved that it wasn't something to do with Candice—where was that girl, anyway?—but she felt terrible for Mr. Devou. Even though he hadn't been very nice the few times that she had spoken to him, he definitely didn't deserve whatever fate had befallen him.

"They don't know yet. I guess his sister was staying with him, and she found his body early this morning. I just thought you should know...people are going to be talking about it all day," he told her. Henry Devou was the richest man in Maple Creek, thanks to his thriving Soup Shoppe. Moira knew that Darrin was right—not much happened in Maple Creek, so this would probably be the talk of the town for the whole week.

"Thanks for letting me know, Darrin. Did you call

Danielle yet? She's working with me today, and I'd rather her hear it from one of us than one of the customers. She used to work for him, you know," Moira said.

"Yeah, I remember. I tried calling her, but she didn't answer. I'll try again a bit later. She might still be sleeping." Darrin chuckled. "Oh, and sorry for waking you up, Ms. D."

"Don't worry about it," Moira told him. "Thanks for letting me know. I'll try calling Danielle too. Poor girl. I know that she and Henry had their differences, but it will still be a shock to her."

Moira got off the phone with Darrin and began her search for Candice. She peeked into her daughter's room, but saw the bed still made. A quick check around the rest of the house showed that her daughter indeed wasn't home. Concerned, Moira dialed Candice's number. She was relieved when her daughter answered on the third ring.

"Mom, I'm so sorry; I forgot to tell you I decided to stay the night at Samantha's," Candice said immediately. "I know you want me to let you know if I'm not coming home for the night... are you mad?"

"No," Moira told her. "I was just worried. I'm glad you're alright. Have fun, and we'll talk later." After hanging up the phone, Moira sank into a kitchen chair and leaned back, closing her eyes. Of course Candice was with Samantha—what else had Moira thought? Why did she feel so uneasy, like something bad was about to happen?

CHAPTER FOUR

Moira got to the deli early again since she hadn't been able to get in touch with Danielle. She was concerned about her young employee. Had she already heard the news? It was with relief when she recognized the small dark-blue sedan parked in the deli's lot. Danielle was already there, and Moira would have a chance to talk to her before they opened up for lunch.

As soon as she saw the young woman, she knew that Danielle had already heard the news about Henry Devou's death. Danielle's face was pale, and her hands were shaking as she greeted Moira. Even though Moira wasn't as close to Danielle as she was to Darrin, she didn't hesitate to take her employee into a comforting hug.

"I'm sorry, Danielle. I know it's a shock. Did Darrin manage to get in touch with you, or did you see it on the news?" Moira asked.

"On... on the news." Danielle's voice was shaky.

"I know it must be hard for you since you worked for him for so long. Do you want to take the day off? I can ask Candice to come in and help if it gets busy," Moira suggested. She wondered if she should close down the store completely today, out of respect for Henry Devou. It was a small enough town that everyone would know what had happened soon enough.

"No, please just let me work like normal today. I need something to take my mind off what happened," the girl said.

"Alright, if that's what you need. You can work in the back so you won't have to talk to the customers. We have to make a new batch of the cheesy herb bread. I'd like to make enough of it to freeze, so that should keep you busy." Moira gave Danielle an encouraging smile. She appreciated the young woman's attitude. She added, "Just let me make the soup of the day, then I'll be out of your hair."

Today's soup was a tomato herb and bisque with quinoa instead of rice. Pretty soon the scents of tomato, garlic, curry, and basil had filled the kitchen. Once the soup was simmering, Moira chopped up some fresh cilantro to use as a garnish, and then stepped back into the main part of the deli to write out the day's specials on the small chalkboard. *Quinoa Tomato Soup and Garlic Grilled Cheese* would be today's sandwich and soup pair. The familiar food with a special twist should be a hit with her customers, and Moira found her own stomach growling as she imagined biting into a grilled cheese sandwich with Amish-made sharp cheddar and sautéed garlic chunks. She realized that she hadn't eaten breakfast yet; a quick glance at the clock showed her that she had just enough time to grab a bowl of soup before the deli opened.

It turned out to be a busier day than Moira had expected. It seemed like every single one of her customers had heard the news about her competitor's death. For some reason, people stared at her for a few seconds longer than usual before ordering. *Do they think it's rude of me to have opened the store today?* she wondered. *Maybe I should have kept it closed out of respect after all. But then Danielle wouldn't have had anything to distract her from being upset.* She couldn't close now anyway, not with a big pot of soup simmering away in the back.

Mary-Lou, one of the more prolific gossips in town, approached the counter with a bottle of sparkling water from the refrigerated section in her hand. She placed the bottle on the counter with more force than necessary and narrowed her eyes at Moira suspiciously. Not sure what she had done to upset the other woman, Moira decided that being polite was the best course of action.

"Is that all?" she asked. "Are you sure you wouldn't like a bowl of soup or a fresh sandwich to go with your drink?"

"No, thank you," Mary-Lou said in an icy voice. "I don't want anything made *in-house.*" Confused, Moira just blinked and rang up the bottle of sparkling water. Why had Mary-Lou even come in if all she wanted was a drink? The deli wasn't anywhere near her house, or near the church that Mary-Lou went to.

"Well, have a nice day." Moira handed the other woman her receipt, and then watched, somewhat hurt, as Mary-Lou walked away without another word. What on earth had gotten into people today?

She was just about to close up for the evening when the door opened. The first customer was a man about her age, with a younger guy following him. Both were bundled up against the cold weather outside. Moira bit her lip, wondering if she had enough soup left for both of them if they were to order some.

"Mrs. Darling?" the older man asked as he approached the counter.

"Ms. Darling," she corrected. "I'm not married. Sorry, do I know you?" She thought that the man looked familiar, but pretty much everyone in town looked familiar, even if she didn't know them by name. He definitely wasn't one of her regulars though. His eyes narrowed as he looked around the deli, taking in the fridge humming in the corner, stocked with artisan drinks and a few containers of prepackaged soup. The clear glass cases contained various breads, some she'd made in the deli and some she'd bought from local businesses. The cheeses and cold cuts were in the refrigerator near the glass cases. Moira was proud that everything she sold was organic and came from local farms and businesses.

"If you have any questions about anything we sell, I'd be happy to answer them. All the cheese is made by our local Amish community." Moira couldn't help but smile as she recited her usual line. Her business was thriving, and she loved knowing that she could be certain of the quality of what she sold.

"I do have a few questions for you, *Ms.* Darling." The man reached into his jacket and pulled out a worn leather wallet. He let it drop open, showing his badge. "I'm Detective Fitzgerald with the Maple Creek police department. This is Detective Jefferson." He nodded at the younger man who stood slightly behind him. "Are you the owner of this establishment?"

"Yes." Moira bit her lip. What was going on? She was certain that all the licensing for Darling's DELIcious Delights was up to date. She always made sure that the deli was in tip-top shape, and couldn't imagine what could have happened to get her in trouble with the police department. The sheriff had come in just last week to pick up some more of his wife's favorite cheese.

"How well did you know Mr. Devou?" The detective had taken a pad of paper out of his pocket and made a quick note on it before looking up at her expectantly. The younger detective was walking around the shop, occasionally bending over to take a closer look at something.

"Not very well," Moira told him. "I'd spoken with him a couple of times. It's a small town, and we're both business owners. You know how it is." Detective Fitzgerald scrawled something on the note pad before speaking again.

"Is the Soup Shoppe direct competition to your store?" he asked.

"Well, only sort of. The Soup Shoppe is more of a restaurant, the sit down and eat type. I'm a deli, so while I do offer fresh sandwiches, salads, and soup, I also sell a lot of prepackaged foods. Quite a few of my customers come here mainly to buy the locally sourced cheeses, meats, and breads that I sell." She offered the detective a tentative smile. "So even if someone eats lunch at the Soup Shoppe, they can still stop here to pick up something for later."

"But it is true that you would likely see an increase in the number of customers that you have if the Soup Shoppe were to close?" The detective tapped the end of his pen against his lips as he waited for her to answer. Moira was beginning to feel uncomfortable with the way he was talking to her. His expression was cold, and he was looking at her with suspicion.

"Yes, a slight increase, but I don't see what that has to do with anything." Moira pursed her lips. "What is this all about?"

"It's routine, ma'am," the other detective, Jefferson, chimed in. "We just need to ask a few questions any time there is a suspicious death." Detective

Fitzgerald shot a glare at the younger detective, but Moira spoke before he could say anything.

"Are you saying you think someone *murdered* Mr. Devou?" She was shocked. She had assumed that the man had suffered some sort of accident, or maybe had a heart attack or something similar. She hadn't had a chance to see the local news, which she was now regretting.

"We're just looking into all the possibilities, ma'am." Detective Fitzgerald made another note on his pad. Moira was beginning to feel that the situation was slipping out of her control. Did these detectives really think that she might have had a hand in a man's death?

"If he was murdered...well, that's terrible. I would never wish that on anyone, even if he *was* putting me out of business. Which he wasn't." She felt tongue tied and confused. She honestly did feel bad that

Henry Devou was dead and hoped the detectives could see that.

"Don't worry, Ms. Darling," Fitzgerald said. "This is just a preliminary investigation. We won't know anything concrete until after we've run a few tests. The only reason we're here is because we found a container of your soup at Mr. Devou's home."

"Well, I hope you find whoever's responsible. Let me know if I can be of any more help," Moira said feeling shocked.

"Thank you. Here's my card. If you think of anything else, please call me. And please let me know if you're going to be leaving the area. We'll be in touch." He gave her a nod then turned on his heel. His companion, Detective Jefferson, smiled apologetically, then followed Fitzgerald.

Once they were both out of the store, Moira hurried

over to lock the front doors, then collapsed into a chair. What had just happened? They couldn't seriously think that she had anything to do with Henry Devou's death, could they? And... why had the owner of the Soup Shoppe had soup from Darling's DELIcious Delights at his house? He had never stopped in for something to eat before, at least not while she was at the counter. Danielle's dark curls appeared in the doorway to the kitchen. She took one look at her boss slouching in the chair and rushed over.

"Are you alright, Ms. D.?" Danielle asked.

"Don't worry, I'm fine," Moira assured her. "I'm just a bit overwhelmed. Two detectives just questioned me. Apparently, Mr. Devou's death was suspicious, and they think I might have had something to do with it."

"Oh." Danielle's face paled. "I'm sure they don't

really think that. I mean, they must question lots of people."

"The older detective, Mr. Fitzgerald, seemed to think that the fact that we were competitors gives me motive." Moira shook her head. "It's just ridiculous. I wouldn't even dream of hurting someone."

"I know, Ms. D." Danielle patted her arm gently. "It will be alright."

CHAPTER FIVE

Despite Danielle's assurances, Moira couldn't help feeling shaken by the incident. It was bad enough that a man might have been murdered. Moira couldn't believe that she was a possible suspect in the eyes of the police. She hoped that they would realize she was innocent as soon as possible. She suddenly remembered how Mary-Lou had behaved earlier, and how even her regular customers had looked at her warily before ordering. Could it be that they had seen the report of Henry Devou's death on the news and had come to the same conclusion that the police had? The thought of her customers suspecting that she might have had something to do with Mr. Devou's death stung.

What she needed to do now was to catch up on the news. She wished she'd asked Darrin more questions when she talked to him that morning, but she had been too worried about Candice to think of it.

When she got home, the first thing she did was switch on the television. She hoped that there would be a rerun of the story that Darrin had seen, but she had no such luck. Moira wasn't one to record the news, so there was no way of viewing any programs from earlier in the day. It looked like the Internet would be her only hope of figuring out what was going on.

A few minutes later, she pulled up a local news website. She clicked on a link with Henry Devou's name in it and began to read. Just as her employee had told her, Henry was found dead by his sister in the early hours of the morning. Moira had never met the man's sister, but she immediately felt terrible for her. *What a horrible thing to have happen*, she thought.

The site reported that police investigations were still pending. There was no information about cause of death, but the reporter did state that an officer had leaked information that led her to believe that the death was suspicious. *So why do people think that I had something to do with it?* Moira wondered. She found her answer in a small blurb at the bottom of the page.

Henry Devou gained local fame last year when his restaurant, the Soup Shoppe, *became a franchise, with various locations opening all over the state in just a few short months. Reports show that his success came at a price to his competitors. At least two local restaurants,* Darling's DELIcious Delights, *and* Arlo's Diner *have reported a loss of customers since the* Soup Shoppe *gained state-wide popularity. A take-home bowl of soup from* Darling's *was found at the scene of the crime, a suspicious find at the house of the deli's competition. Could Henry Devou's death have been a last-ditch ploy to save a dying business? Is there a murderer walking the sleepy streets of Maple Creek? Subscribe to our email list to keep up to date with the latest news about the death of Henry Devou.*

Moira stared at the screen for a moment, her eyes narrowed. Who had told the Maple Creek News that her deli was losing customers? While she had been getting in slightly fewer customers than usual, the difference hadn't been enough to affect business much. As she had told the detective, her deli was more than just a soup and sandwich shop, and it was doing just fine, thank you very much. This article made it sound like she was being put out of business by the Soup Shoppe, which was just not true.

In addition to manipulating the facts to make it sound like the deli was in trouble, the website also seemed to imply that she and Arlo were possible murder suspects. Moira was fuming. As far as she could tell, the police hadn't even released any official reports about Devou's death. All the reporters were doing right now was fear mongering, which wasn't fair to her *or* Arlo—a sixty-year-old man who had owned the small diner on Main Street for over half his life. *Maybe I should call them and complain,* Moira thought.

She started looking for the *Maple Creek News* telephone number when she heard a key in the front door. A moment later, the door opened and she heard Candice call out, "Mom?"

"In here, sweetie," Moira called back. She could deal with the bad publicity from the news later. Right now, she wanted to spend some quality time with her daughter—and catch Candice up on the day's events.

CHAPTER SIX

"Wow, Danielle, this is delicious." Moira took another bite of the sandwich her employee had surprised her with. The toasted olive bread crunched as she bit into it, then the savory flavors of roast beef, caramelized onions, melted swiss cheese, and steak sauce flooded her mouth.

"I thought it would go well with a French onion soup. Maybe we could serve it later this week." Danielle bit her lip. "If you think it's good enough, of course. It's just something I whipped up this morning. I was feeling creative."

"I think it will be perfect." Moira gave her employee

an encouraging smile. "Do you think you can make another couple of these? We can try them out on Darrin and Candice when they come in."

"Sure, I'll get started right away." Danielle beamed at her and then hurried back into the kitchen. Moira was glad to see such enthusiasm from the young woman. Ever since Henry Devou's death, she had been unusually withdrawn and emotional. A quick peek through the swinging door showed Danielle humming to herself as she worked. The sight of her eagerly slicing roast beef was definitely an improvement from her demeanor just a few days ago.

Moira decided to let Danielle work in peace and returned to the counter. There was a lull between customers, and she took the opportunity to straighten up. Keeping the store tidy seemed to be a never ending job, but it was one that she didn't mind.

She was crouching in front of the cheese section,

trying to figure out how on earth the packages of swiss had gotten mixed in with the white cheddar when she heard the front door open. She looked over her shoulder with a smile on her face, ready to greet a customer, and was surprised to see the familiar face of Detective Fitzgerald looking down at her. Moira stood up quickly, self-consciously straightening her apron as she turned to face him.

"Can I help you?" she asked, keeping her tone polite even though just seeing the detective set her on edge.

"I would like to ask you some more questions, Ms. Darling, if you don't mind. Can you accompany me to the station?" he asked.

"Right now?" Moira frowned. "It's the middle of my business hours, detective. We're just about to get our evening rush. I really can't leave the store right now." Detective Fitzgerald sighed and looked around at the empty store.

"How about I ask you a few questions here, and then you come down to the station later if we need to ask you anything else, does that work for you?" he asked.

"Yes, thank you." She glanced outside, but the younger detective was nowhere in sight. If she had to answer more questions, she would rather talk to Jefferson; he had seemed like the nicer of the two. "Um, would you like something to eat or drink?" She almost added *it's on the house*, but at the last moment, she realized that it might sound like she was trying to bribe him.

"No, thank you." He gestured to the nearest table. "Please take a seat Ms. Darling. This won't take long." Moira sat down, her mouth suddenly dry. She hadn't done anything wrong, so why did she feel so nervous?

"Where were you last Saturday evening?" He

touched his pen to his notepad and looked up at her expectantly.

"I was at home," she said, thinking back. "Well, actually, I went shopping after work, and then I went home."

"Where did you go shopping?" he asked.

"Tulman's Fresh Market," she said, naming the local grocery store. "I was buying some things for dinner."

"Did you go anywhere after you went home?" He made a note.

"No. I stayed in all night. I watched some television and then went to bed." She hesitated, then decided that it would probably be safe to ask him a question of her own. "Have I done something wrong, Detective Fitzgerald?"

"I'm just gathering information, Ms. Darling. Nothing to worry about." He held her gaze until she looked away and then continued with his questioning. "Is there anyone that can confirm your whereabouts for last Saturday evening?"

"Well, the cashier at the store would probably remember me being there. Her name's Rachel, she's a friend of my daughter from when they were in high school," Moira told him.

"How about after you left? Can anyone confirm that you were at your house?" He tapped the pen against his lips, a mannerism that she remembered from the last time he had questioned her.

"No," she said, remembering with a sinking feeling in her gut. "Candice, my daughter, lives with me, but she spent last Saturday night at a friend's house."

"Hmm." Detective Fitzgerald took a few more notes and then slipped his pen back into his pocket. "That's all for now, Ms. Darling. We'll be in contact with you if we need anything else." He glanced at his notepad. "Do you have any employees in today?"

"Yes, Danielle is in the back." Moira straightened in her seat. "But please try not to be too hard on her. She's been very upset by all this."

The detective raised an eyebrow but only said, "Could you please send her out?" Reluctantly, Moira rose from her chair to go find her employee. She didn't like the thought of Danielle being interviewed by the stern detective, but she knew that there was nothing she could do about it.

"Did he say why he wanted to talk to you guys?" Darrin asked. The sandwich that Danielle made for him was sitting untouched on his plate. She had just closed the store for the evening, and the four of them—her, Danielle, Darrin, and Candice—were

41

sitting in the dining area together. Soon after hiring Danielle, Moira had started a tradition of having employee dinner meetings once a week where she supplied a free dinner, and they all got a chance to talk about business and plan the next week's specials. Normally the topic of conversation stayed on food, but tonight they had gotten sidetracked when Moira mentioned Detective Fitzgerald's visit.

"No." Moira shook her head. "He just asked me where I was the night that Henry Devou died and then told me he'd be in contact if he needed anything else. Did he explain anything when he talked to you?" She glanced over at Danielle, who shook her head.

"Nope, he just said the same things as he said to you. He asked where I had been, and if I had anyone who could confirm it." Danielle's eyes darted over to Darrin, and then away again. The motion was so quick that Moira thought she must have imagined it.

"Do you think that detective is going to question Darrin and me too?" Candice asked.

"I don't know, Candice. But there's nothing to worry about if he does. Just be yourself and answer truthfully." Moira gave her daughter what she hoped was a reassuring smile.

"So, have they decided that Devou's death was actually a murder?" Darrin looked around at the rest of them. "I mean, the police wouldn't be questioning people if he had like, had a heart attack or something, would they?"

"I doubt it," Moira said. "I don't know much about how this stuff works though. Maybe something will be on the news tomorrow." She shook her head. "A murder in Maple Creek. Things like that just don't happen here. If someone *did* kill Henry Devou, I hope they catch him quickly. The thought of a murderer in town is just terrifying."

43

CHAPTER SEVEN

At first, Moira thought the pounding was part of a dream, but she quickly realized that it was the sound of someone knocking on the door. Knocking *loudly*. She stumbled out of bed and pulled on her bathrobe as she stepped into the hallway. Candice poked her head around her bedroom door, her brown eyes wide.

"Who is it?" she asked.

"I've got no idea." Moira hesitated at the top of the stairs. "You stay up here, alright?" She remembered the conversation from last night. The talk of killing and murderers had put her on edge. Candice

45

nodded, biting her lip in concern before ducking back into her bedroom. The pounding came again, as Moira made her way down the steps.

She opened the front door to find two uniformed police officers on her porch.

"Moira Darling?" one of them asked.

"Yes, that's me," she said. "What can I do for you?"

"We're going to need you to come down to the station."

"Am I… am I under arrest?" The two officers traded a glance, then the one who had been speaking shook his head.

"No, you're not. We just need to ask you some questions," he told her.

"Is it alright if I get dressed first?" Moira glanced down at her bathrobe. She really didn't want to go down to the police station in her pajamas.

"Go ahead," the officer said. "We'll wait for you out here." She hurried upstairs where Candice was waiting by her bedroom door. Her daughter had taken the time to get fully dressed and was looking at Moira with concern.

"I heard everything," she said to her mother. "Why do they need to question you?"

"I don't know, but I'm sure it's just normal procedure." Moira gave her daughter a reassuring smile. "Can you go to the deli for me if I'm not back before it opens? Tell Darrin that all the ingredients for the soup of the day are in the fridge and that we need to order more of the bread and butter pickles."

"Of course I'll go to the deli. I'll help out however I can, and I'm sure Darrin and I can call Danielle in if we need more help. But what about you, Mom? Do you want me to call anyone? What if they, I don't know, arrest you or something?" Candice bit her lip, concern making her look even younger than she was.

"I'll be fine, sweetheart. If you get too worried, you can always call your father. I know he and I don't get along very well, but he does love you." She glanced down the stairs. "I'd better get dressed, Candice. They're waiting for me."

Moira followed the officers down to the station, relieved that she had been able to drive her own car. She wondered what was going on. Why did the police keep questioning her about Henry Devou? She knew that she was innocent, but she couldn't help feeling like she had done something wrong whenever she spoke to the police. She hoped that they weren't questioning Danielle as much as they were questioning her. The poor girl didn't need thoughts of her former boss's death dragged up again and again.

"Right this way, ma'am." Moira followed the officer as he led her down one of Maple Creek Police Department's hallways. She couldn't believe that an hour ago, she had been asleep in her bed. Now she was about to be questioned by the police for the third time, and she hadn't even had her coffee yet.

"Through here." The officer opened a door for her. As Moira walked past him, he added, "It will probably be a few minutes." It was a small room, with blank walls and a simple square table that had a few metal chairs set up around it. There was no two-way mirror, but she could see a camera on the ceiling. She pulled out one of the chairs and sat down, keeping her coat on since the room was chilly. She hoped Candice wasn't too worried; she would call her daughter the second she got out of here. Then she would see if Danielle could meet them at the deli—it looked like they might need to have another staff meeting. If Henry Devou's death *was* somehow linked to the deli, her employees deserved to know.

She quickly became bored just sitting at the table, so she began planning new soup recipes. She tried to come up with a few new soup and sandwich combos each month, to keep things interesting for her customers, and herself. During the busy summer months, she usually had a couple of different soups available, but there usually weren't enough customers during the winter to have more than one pot of soup boiling at a time. Of course, she offered prepackaged versions of some of her most popular soups and offered catering services when someone asked her, though she didn't advertise them.

Maybe I can do some sort of beef stew next, Moira thought. Hearty recipes sold best during the cold winter months, and stews always went over well. *Yes, beef stew, with lots of carrots, pearl onions, and rosemary. Should I do potatoes or dumplings?* Beef Dumpling Stew sounded good to her, but she would have to play around with the dumpling recipe a little bit and add some seasonal spices.

She was so involved with imagining what flavors would make the stew just perfect that she jumped when the door to the interview room opened. Detective Fitzgerald and Detective Jefferson walked in, the latter carrying two cups of coffee. He placed one in front of her, the rich scent going to her head and reminding her that she hadn't had anything to eat or drink yet.

"I can get you sugar or cream to go with that, if you'd like," said the detective.

"No, thanks." Moira wrapped her hand around the warm mug. While she didn't usually like the taste of black coffee, she knew that the bitter taste would help keep her alert.

"I'm sorry that we asked you to come down to the

station so early, but we didn't want to disturb you while you were at work." Detective Jefferson sat down across from her, and Detective Fitzgerald sat next to him. The older detective nodded in greeting, but said nothing.

"Do you know why you're here?" Jefferson asked.

"No, not really," she admitted. "One of the officers that picked me up said that you wanted to ask me more questions. I'm guessing it has something to do with Henry Devou, but I don't know why or what I could possibly do to help."

"When was the last time you saw Mr. Devou, Ms. Darling?" The detective took a sip of his own coffee, gazing at her calmly as he waited for her to answer his question.

"Um, I'm not sure." She thought back, trying to remember when she last had a run-in with her competitor. "A few months ago, I guess? During the fair in June. We both had tables for the food contest."

"Did you win?"

"No, he did." She smiled at the memory of the fair. It had been hot out, but with a gentle breeze. She and Darrin had been working the table; Candice had been out of town with some of her friends, and she hadn't hired Danielle yet. In fact, she remembered seeing Danielle at the Soup Shoppe's table. Even though she hadn't won the contest, it had been a fun experience, and one that she was eager to repeat next year.

"How did you feel about that?" he asked.

"Oh, it was fun. It was a fair contest, and his soup was great," she admitted.

"And you haven't seen him since?"

"I don't think so. I mean, I might have gotten a glimpse of him at the grocery store, or while I was out driving. It's a small town." She shrugged. "But I haven't spoken to him since the fair."

"Not even on the night of his death? Saturday night?"

"No. Like I told you before, I bought groceries and then I went home."

"Did Devou come into your restaurant before you left?"

"He never comes to the deli. Saturday night wasn't any different." Moira frowned. "What is this all about?"

"Ms. Darling, does your restaurant do deliveries?" Jefferson asked, ignoring her question.

"We don't deliver," she said. "We do catering sometimes, but only after hours. It's not something we advertise." The detective raised an eyebrow.

"Well, did you *cater* to Henry Devou's house that evening?" he asked.

"We haven't had any catering jobs since November. You can check our schedule." Sighing, she asked, "Will you please tell me why I'm in here? I really don't have any idea what's going on."

"A takeout container from your deli was found at Henry Devou's house, Ms. Darling. It had the remnants of soup from your store in it."

"I have no idea why he would have bought soup

from the deli, and I just don't understand what that
has to do with me or my employees."

"Henry Devou was poisoned, Ms. Darling," the other
detective, Fitzgerald cut in. "And your soup was the
last thing that he ate."

CHAPTER EIGHT

Moira was shocked speechless. Henry Devou had been poisoned? Who would have killed him? She had no doubt that the man had enemies, but things like this just didn't happen in Maple Creek. It took her a moment to wrap her mind around the fact that someone she knew had been murdered. Even though she didn't like him very much; he was rude, obnoxious, and didn't seem to care who he stepped on to get to the top, it was a shock. Finally, she realized the real implications of what the detective had just said.

"Wait, are you saying that you think *I* poisoned him?"

"We're just gathering information, Ms. Darling." Jefferson made a calming motion with his hands. "We're still investigating the crime. You're a person of interest right now. I'm going to have to ask you not to leave town without talking to me first. As long as you cooperate with us, this will all be over soon enough. Is that understood?" Moira nodded, still in shock.

"Am I... am I under arrest?" she asked in a quiet voice.

"No ma'am, not at this time."

"Can I go then? My daughter... she'll be worried about me." Moira was sick at the thought of what she was going to tell Candice. Henry Devou had been murdered, and the police were pointing fingers at the deli.

"Just a few more questions, Ms. Darling, and then you can be on your way."

Moira went straight from the police station to the deli where she was relieved to find Candice and Darrin already preparing for the day. Candice took one look at her mother's face and rushed over.

"What is it, Mom? What happened?" she asked. Darrin followed slowly behind her, concern creasing his forehead. Moira felt tears prick her eyes at the sight of their worried faces. Her world might be falling apart around her, but at least she still had the love and support of her family and friends.

She waited until Danielle arrived to tell the three of them her story. They were silent as she spoke, with Candice chewing on her lower lip and Darrin's frown getting deeper and deeper. Danielle was pale and kept closing her eyes as if in disbelief. Moira knew that what she was saying might affect all of them. If the police seriously thought that Henry Devou had been poisoned by something from the deli, then they all would be considered suspects.

"I just don't know what to do," she said finally. "None of it makes any sense. Why would Henry Devou have a container of soup from here? And why would he die right after eating it?"

"Did they say if they had actually found poison in the soup?" Darrin asked.

"Well, no," she said. "They said they were still investigating. I just don't understand why he was eating our soup in the first place. He was always so rude about everything we sold. He wouldn't even taste it at the fair last summer." She paused. "Do any of you remember seeing him in here?" Each of her employees shook their heads. Moira frowned, trying to think of a plausible explanation for how her competitor died eating a bowl of her Soup of the Day.

"Maybe it was planted there by whoever actually

killed him," Candice said after a moment. Moira glanced at her daughter. Normally she wouldn't even consider something like that she kept telling herself, these sorts of things just didn't happen in Maple Creek. But the truth was, someone had been murdered. It felt like anything might be true now.

"It makes sense," her daughter continued. "The whole town knows that you've been losing customers since his business began growing. That gives you a reason to kill him, at least as far as some people are concerned."

Darrin nodded. "Motive."

"And now the police will be busy investigating us instead of looking into whoever actually did it," her daughter continued. "You should get a lawyer, Mom."

"I don't know… wouldn't that make me look guilty?" Moira asked. Candice shrugged.

"One of my friends from college, his dad is a lawyer. I can send him a message I guess." Her daughter glanced at her phone. "But Jason won't be up yet. He works night shifts."

"Just ask him if he thinks I should get a lawyer right now, or wait for this to blow over." Moira sighed. "I just want this whole thing to be over."

"Ms. D., I've got an idea," Darrin cut in. "I know a guy in Lake Marion who does private detective work. Like, private investigator stuff. Since the police are busy investigating you, he might be able to find out who actually killed the guy."

"I'm not supposed to leave town without letting the police know," she said with a grimace.

"I'm sure he'd be willing to meet you in Maple Creek," he replied.

"Do you really think I'll need him? Wouldn't it be better just to let the police do their thing?" She didn't like the idea of doing anything that would draw more attention to herself. She was innocent. Surely the police investigating Henry Devou's murder would be able to see that.

"You know I didn't grow up around here, Ms. D.. My family didn't live in the best part of the city. I've seen people get arrested for things that they didn't do. I'm sure things are different in a small town like this, but it still can't hurt to have someone on your side looking into things, can it?" he asked.

"I guess not. Alright, I'll give your friend a call." Moira looked around at her employees and daughter gratefully. "Thank you, everyone. It really means a lot that you're trying to help me out—Danielle, are you alright?" The young woman was visibly shaking, and her face was pale.

"I don't feel very good," she mumbled.

"Oh, sweetie, I'm sorry. You should have said something earlier. Go on and head home. We'll manage from here." She was never one to make her employees work if they were sick, and this wasn't even a day that Danielle was scheduled. Moira felt bad for being so involved in her story that she hadn't noticed how ill the young woman looked.

Danielle nodded and rose. She gathered her purse and coat, and a moment later was out the door and walking towards her small, blue car. Darrin was watching her go with a slight frown on his face, but his expression cleared when Candice spoke again.

"Don't worry, Mom. We'll figure this out." She gave her mother a reassuring smile. "I'm going to go make sure everything is ready for the day. We're supposed to open in ten minutes." Moira glanced at the clock, shocked to see how much time had passed. It was indeed almost time for the deli to open, and she hadn't even written the special down on the chalkboard yet.

"Well, we'd better get to work," she said. "I'll take care of the register. I want our customers to see that we have nothing to hide."

CHAPTER NINE

At first, Moira wasn't worried when no customers came in. It was a chilly, gray day with occasional snow flurries. The roads were bad, and she didn't blame her customers for wanting to stay home. But when four o'clock came, and their only customers had been an elderly man who stopped in every week for a fresh log of salami and a wedge of smoked cheddar cheese and a couple driving through Maple Creek on their way to the Mackinac Bridge, she began to wonder if something else was going on.

"Hey, Darrin," she said when he stepped out of the kitchen for his break. "You can head home if you want to. It doesn't make sense to have all three of us here when it's so slow."

"Alright, Ms. D., thanks. Oh, here's that guy's number, the private investigator that I was telling you about." He took a folded piece of paper out of his pocket and set it on the counter next to her. "His name is David Morris. He taught criminal justice at my college for a semester."

"I'll think about it." She gave a small laugh. "I'm going to feel pretty silly if it turns out that I'm overreacting. They could catch the real murderer tomorrow."

Darrin had only been gone for a few minutes when Candice poked her head out of the kitchen. "Hey, Mom, you should see this." She had her phone out, and a worried expression on her face.

"What is it?" Moira moved next to her daughter so she could look over her shoulder. The phone's screen showed an article from the local news website. *Local Deli Serves Up More Than Soup,* read the headline.

"I think I know why no one's coming in today," her daughter said.

"How do they know this?" Moira asked after reading through the article which detailed how a bowl of soup from Darling's DELIcious Delights had been the last thing that Henry Devou had eaten before he died. While the article didn't directly say that Moira had poisoned him, the implication was obvious. "Aren't the police supposed to keep this sort of information secret, at least until they have proof?"

"No idea," Candice said. "But if people think you poisoned someone, no one's going to come in."

"I think that maybe you and Darrin are right," she told her daughter at last. "We do need outside help. The sooner this gets solved, the better. The store can't survive many more days like this." The dull day was interrupted only once more. Moira was sitting at the counter when the front door slammed open, and an angry woman strode in. She was maybe a decade older than Moira, with long hair that had gone mostly gray, and a stern face that looked slightly familiar, although she couldn't place it.

"Hello," she began. "Welcome to…"

"How dare you?" the woman cut her off. "You murderer! How can you sit there with a smile on your face?" Her voice was high and loud with emotion. She approached the counter, shaking a stiff finger in Moira's face. "If I didn't know that the police were doing everything in their power to bring you in, I would deal with you myself. You horrible, horrible woman, I hope you rot in a cell for the rest of your life."

Moira sat stunned, through this tirade. The verbal attack was so sudden and so harsh that she was frozen. As the woman took a deep breath to fuel her next rage-filled sentences, Candice ran out of the kitchen with her cell phone in hand.

"What's going on here?" she asked, wide-eyed. The woman turned to her and began yelling again, even louder. This attack on her daughter snapped Moira out of it. She snatched Candice's phone out of her hand and held it up like a weapon.

"Get out of my store this second, or I'm calling the police," she said. The woman glared and scowled at both of them, but reluctantly turned and left. Trading a glance with her daughter, she saw that Candice was just as stunned as she was. What on earth had just happened? It looked like she really did need some help.

CHAPTER TEN

"Thanks for meeting me here." David Morris looked up as Moira approached the table. Her bright green eyes curious as she took him in. He was wearing a trench coat, even though it was a bit clichéd. It fit him well.

"Not a problem, I need more excuses to get out of town." He extended a hand. "David Morris, private investigator."

She shook his hand, and then introduced herself, "Moira Darling, deli owner." She gave him a quick smile.

"So, what can I do for you, Ms. Darling?" he asked. Before she answered him, she looked around to make sure no one that knew her was nearby. They were meeting at a chain coffee shop right on the edge of Maple Creek, the halfway point between their two towns. As soon as she seemed confident that no one was listening in, she leaned forward and began her story.

"...and now no one is coming to the deli, and the police think *I* killed someone," she finished.

"Did you?" he asked.

"No!" Moira blushed and lowered her voice. "Sorry, I didn't mean to shout. But how could you think that?"

"I'm just making sure," he said. "Have you spoken to anyone else about this?"

"Just my employees and my daughter," she told him.

"And what exactly is it that you want me to do?" He took a sip of his coffee as he waited for her to answer. Some people seemed to think that private investigators had superpowers and expected him to do impossible things.

"Just... look around. Find out who actually killed Mr. Devou. As long as people think I did it, they aren't going to come to my deli. If this goes on for long enough, I'll be put out of business." She paused. "So, will you take the case?"

"I will. And I can't promise anything, but I'll do my best to prove your innocence as soon as I can, Ms. Darling," he said.

"Please, call me Moira," she told him.

He watched, bemused, as Moira Darling left the coffee shop and drove away. He didn't know how a nice lady like her had gotten mixed up in a murder, but he did know that he wanted to help her out of it. While he doubted that she was in any real danger of being arrested for a crime that she didn't commit, he could understand the effect that it was having on her business. He knew firsthand how gossipy and cliquey these small towns could be.

This had come at the perfect time for him. Business was slow; lately it seemed that all he had been getting in was cases about cheating spouses and small-time thievery. It had been too long since he'd had a case he could really sink his teeth into. He had been thinking of relocating, moving to a bigger city, where there would hopefully be more cases for him to work on.

But for now, he would start out by doing some reconnaissance at the dead guy's restaurant, the Soup Shoppe. After that, well, he would see where things took him.

CHAPTER ELEVEN

"I met with that private investigator yesterday,"
Moira told Danielle as she grated cheese for her Five
Cheese, Five Star soup. She found herself grinning
as she remembered the handsome man who looked
just like she imagined a private investigator should
look, with a long trench coat and distinguished salt-
and-pepper hair. With shockingly blue eyes, the
detective was definitely handsome. Danielle glanced
over at her, her gloved hands pausing on the turkey
breast that she was slicing.

"What did he say?" she asked.

"He agreed to take the case. He said that he'd call me

once he turned something up." She paused to dump the pile of grated cheese into the pot on the stove where it would slowly melt as she stirred it. The trick was not to let the mixture boil, otherwise, the cheese would curdle, and she would have to start over. "Hopefully today is busier than the last few days have been; Candice is getting tired of eating leftover soup."

"Yeah, hopefully," her employee said. "But the detective... did he tell you what he was going to do? Like, what does he look at when he's investigating something? What sort of track record does he have?"

"Well, Candice and I looked at his website before I met with him. It had an area where previous customers could leave comments, and they all seemed only to have good things to say about him. I'm not sure exactly how he investigates things, but he definitely seems smart." *And handsome* but she kept that part to herself. "Don't worry, I'm sure that between him and the police, they'll find out who poisoned Henry Devou."

Moira's hopes that today would be busier than the past couple of days didn't last. The deli remained silent and empty long after she had flipped the sign on the door from *Closed* to *Open*. She passed the time by reading a novel and snacking on small bowls of the decadently rich cheese soup that she had made. Five different types of cheese, hearty chunks of cauliflower, and cubed ham made for a tasty, if fattening, meal. She was debating making herself a Sandwich of the Day to go along with the soup— ham and turkey on flat bread, with melted cheddar and baby spinach leaves—when the door to the deli opened and in walked David Morris.

"Did you find something already?" she asked eagerly.

"Nothing major, I'm sorry to say," he told her. "I just came from the Soup Shoppe—I thought I could ask around there and see if any of the people who worked for him knew who would want to kill him."

"Did you find anything out? Oh, and can I offer you anything? The daily special is on the board, and we've got drinks in the fridge." Moira looked around at the empty store. "We sure could use the business."

"No, thanks." Much to her surprise, the private investigator actually looked embarrassed. "I ate at the Soup Shoppe."

"Oh." She felt deflated. Even the detective that she had hired didn't want to eat at her restaurant.

"And as far as what I found out, well, it seems as if no one really liked the guy. None of his employees had anything good to say about him. They all agree that he was rude, demanding, and unfair. There definitely isn't a shortage of people with motive to kill him. Any one of his employees or other competitors might have wanted to see him dead," he told her.

"Okay, but why would any of them want to frame

me?" she asked. "As far as I know, I don't have any enemies."

"It might not be personal." David shrugged. "Whoever did it might have just thought that you would be an easy target to frame for murder since you have a plausible motive. There's also the possibility that this is all a very bad coincidence."

"How could it be a coincidence, Mr. Morris? Someone obviously planted the bowl of soup from my deli at his house and mixed in the poison that they used to kill him."

"Just because you and your employees don't remember serving Mr. Devou the weekend of his death doesn't mean that the soup was planted. His sister was staying with him if I remember correctly. It's possible that she could have stopped at your deli to pick up something to eat." He hesitated for a moment, then added, "There's also the possibility that one of your employees could be lying about seeing him."

"Why would they lie about that? No, I trust each of my employees completely." She shook her head. "I'm telling you, none of us sold anything to Henry Devou. I'm not sure about his sister—I've never met the lady, and couldn't tell you if I had seen her or not."

"If I get a picture of her, would you be willing to show it to your employees and your daughter and ask them if they recognize her?" he asked.

"Yes, I don't see why not," she said.

"I'll see if I can find a picture of her online and print it off. One more thing," he said. "Is it alright if I take a look around the deli after you close for the evening? If you're right and someone is trying to frame you for the murder, they may very well have planted evidence here as well."

"Of course, that's fine. I have nothing to hide." She gave him a grateful smile. "Thanks again for taking this case."

"It's my pleasure." He nodded at her and then turned to leave. "I'll be back in a couple of hours with a picture of the sister," he added. "And if you can keep the fact that I'm going to look around the deli quiet, that would be great. I know you trust your employees, but at this point, we can't fully trust anyone."

CHAPTER TWELVE

David pulled up in front of Darling's DELIcious Delights a few hours later with a freshly printed picture of Mathilda Devou, the victim's spinster sister. The more he thought about it, the more plausible the idea of the sister being the killer seemed to be. She was older than her brother, but nowhere near as successful. From what he had seen, jealousy could be a pretty good motivator for a crime.

Besides that, as far as he could tell, she was the Henry Devou's only living relative. Since Devou wasn't married and didn't have any kids, chances were the sister would be inheriting everything. In fact, Mathilda Devou was such a perfect suspect that he wondered why the police were focusing on Moira instead of her. He was starting to understand why the attractive, independent owner of the deli had seemed so worried when she had first spoken to him about the case. Something definitely didn't seem right here.

David got out of the car, locked it, and then headed into the store. It was just a few minutes before closing time, and he was sorry to see that the store was just as empty now as it had been when he had come in earlier. Moira looked up from a sheaf of papers as the door shut behind him and offered him a quick smile.

"I was beginning to think you weren't going to make it in before we closed," she said.

"Well, I'm glad I made it in time. I have a recent picture of Mathilda Devou, if you're ready to take a look at it." He slid the picture across the glass counter towards her. She only had to glance at it before she shuddered and turned her face away, pushing the picture back towards him.

"I recognize her!" she said. "She came in yesterday and yelled at my daughter and me. She said horrible things. But that was days after Henry died. I'd never seen her before that."

"You can keep it. Show it to your employees and see if one of them recognizes her."

"I will. Actually, one of my employees, Danielle, is here right now. Hold on, I'll go get her." The deli owner rose from her chair and slipped through the door that led to the kitchen. A moment later she reappeared with a young woman who had curly brown hair and a nervous expression.

"This is Danielle," Moira said. "She used to work for Henry Devou at the Soup Shoppe. She's been with me for almost six months." Turning to her employee, she said, "Mr. Morris just wants to ask you if you recognize someone. It will only take a second, then you can head home."

"Do you remember seeing this woman come in at all during the week before Devou's death?" David turned the picture of Mathilda Devou so it was facing Danielle.

"I... I think she does look familiar," she said after looking at the photo for quite a few seconds. "Yeah, in fact, I'm almost positive it was her that I sold our last bowl of soup to on Saturday." David and Moira traded a glance over Danielle's head. This was looking more promising by the second.

"How sure are you that it was her? Do you remember anything else about her?"

"No, I'm sorry. It was late, and it had been a busy day. I'm pretty sure it was the same lady as in the photo, but I can't, you know, swear to it." The young woman gave a nervous laugh and then looked at her boss. "Sorry, Ms. D., I wish I could be of more help."

"That's alright, Danielle. I know this has been hard for you. You can head home now. I'll see you in a couple of days," said Moira.

After the young employee had gathered her stuff and left the store, David turned to Moira. She was looking at him expectantly, her bright green eyes hopeful.

"What do you think?" she asked. "Can we tell the police what we found out?"

"Not yet. I know you trust your employees, but we don't actually have any proof that Devou's sister was here. Danielle wasn't exactly certain that she recognized her," he told her. "You don't happen to have security cameras, do you?"

"No." She sighed. "Darrin keeps telling me I should install them, but I haven't done it yet."

"It's a good idea." He glanced out the window, making a mental note to check with the surrounding shops and see if they had any outdoor cameras that looked into the deli's parking lot.

"I'd still like to take a look around, if that's okay with you," he said.

"Of course. Do you want me to stay or go?" she asked.

"I'd prefer to look around on my own, but if you want to stay here for security reasons, I understand," he said.

"No, that's fine. I'll run to the store and get a few last-minute things for dinner and then come back and lock up." She looked around at the front room of her deli. "But please try to keep things neat."

"I won't leave a mess. I promise."

An hour later, he met Moira at the door. He didn't know whether it was good or bad that he hadn't found anything of note in the deli during his search. On one hand, if the police somehow managed to get a warrant to search the premises, at least he and Moira could be sure that they wouldn't find any incriminating evidence planted by whoever was trying to set her up. On the other hand, if someone *had* planted something in her store and he had found it, it might have given them a clue as to who the murderer was.

While David still thought that the sister was a likely candidate, he knew that there wasn't any real evidence tying her to Henry Devou's death. If only the deli owner had installed security cameras, then they might have something to go on. At least he had gotten pictures of her employees' schedule and recent receipts. *Someone* had to have gotten the bowl of soup from Moira's deli, his job was to find out who.

"Find anything?" she asked as she locked the front door of the deli behind him.

"Sorry, no. I've got some things to look over tonight though, and I'll question a couple of other people tomorrow." He gave her his best reassuring smile. "Don't worry. We'll find something sooner or later."

CHAPTER THIRTEEN

"What has that private detective found so far?" Candice asked as she served herself the last helping of mashed potatoes. Moira and her daughter were finishing up a late dinner together, and both of them had been unusually silent so far. Moira looked up from the small pile of peas that she had been pushing around her plate and caught her daughter up on what had happened earlier that day.

"...So, we don't really have much," she finished. "Henry Devou's sister *might* have stopped at the store Saturday evening, but Danielle isn't certain. Devou was poisoned, and the police think that a bowl of my soup did it. According to David, it could take them days or even weeks to figure out what poisoned him and to match it to the samples of the soup that they took at the scene. I don't know what we're going to do if business stays this bad for that long. No one wants to buy lunch from someone they think is a killer." She sighed and propped up her head with one hand as she halfheartedly stabbed at a pea with her fork. "Maybe I should just close down the deli now. Someone used my soup to kill someone. Even though I didn't do it, it's partially my fault."

"That's just silly, Mom. Don't blame yourself for this. We all know you're innocent, and the other employees and I all support you. We can have another staff meeting and make a list of everyone that we remember selling soup to on Saturday. It shouldn't be that hard—not all of our customers even bought soup, and we only have to try to remember people who bought soup to go, which narrows the list down even further," her daughter said.

"I guess it's worth a try." Moira paused, struck by the feeling that there was something that she should be noticing. "Saturday..." she murmured. Candice gave her an inquisitive look.

"Candice..." she began slowly. "The police told me that there was a half-eaten bowl of chicken noodle soup next to Henry, when he was found. We served Leeky Soup on Saturday, not chicken noodle. We served that on Friday. We've been going over the wrong day. Whoever bought the soup bought it on Friday." She was amazed that she hadn't realized this before. "And I have an alibi for Friday evening; I spent it with you, remember? That was the day we went to Arlo's for burgers after work."

"Yeah, I remember. And Danny was working there— I went to school with him, he'll remember us for sure." She grinned at her mother. "I mean it's not perfect; since Henry didn't die until Saturday, you could have gotten the soup to him at any time between Friday and Saturday evening, but it's definitely something."

"I've got to tell David." Moira glanced at her watch. It was just before nine o'clock. It would probably be okay to call him if she did it now.

Excusing herself from the table, she slipped into the kitchen and grabbed her cell phone.

David answered on the second ring. Moira quickly told him what she had realized—that whoever had bought the soup used to poison Henry Devou had done it on Friday instead of Saturday.

"I've been going over the wrong day," he said with a groan. "I took pictures of your stack of receipts while I was looking around the deli. I've been making a list of everyone who bought a bowl of soup to go with a credit card and searching for them online to see if they had any connection to Devou. It's pretty incomplete, since you didn't print out cash receipts, but I thought I might get lucky."

"Sorry," she said. "I should have made the connection earlier."

"It's not your fault; this is my job. I have a picture of your employee schedule right here, which has the daily specials written on it. It was right here in front of my face the whole time and I didn't notice it." He gave a dry laugh. "Some investigator I am."

"You've been doing great," Moira assured him. "You realized that his sister had motive to kill him, and she's still our most likely suspect, isn't she?"

"Absolutely. While a lot of people might have had a reason to dislike Henry Devou, his older sister is definitely the one that would benefit the most from his death. Do you still have that picture of her?" he asked.

"Yes, it's in my purse," she told him.

"Great, can you show it to your other employees and see if they recognize her? I'll start going over the receipts from Friday." He sighed. "I doubt that she paid with a credit card, but you never know."

"Candice said she only remembers her from that day she came in yelling at us and I'll let you know if Darrin recognizes the picture of Mathilda," she promised. "Good luck. Hopefully one of us will turn something up."

CHAPTER FOURTEEN

Darrin didn't recognize Mathilda from the picture, so Moira was back at square one when she went into work the next morning. The fact that David hadn't called her meant that he probably hadn't found anything, either.

She had one customer early in the morning, then saw no one else for almost an hour. She was reading a magazine when she heard the front door open.

"It smells like heaven in here," a familiar voice called out. Moira looked up to see the elderly diner owner, Arlo, standing at the entrance to the diner.

"Come on in," she said. "I was just about to take a break for lunch. Care to join me?" He paused, his expression unsure.

"It's on the house," she added.

"Then count me in." He gave her a grateful smile and walked forward to lean against the counter. Moira knew that his business had been hit hard by the Soup Shoppe. Arlo's Diner had been the most popular sit-down restaurant in town before Henry Devou had opened his business just a few blocks away from the diner. She suspected that the diner was now in trouble. Arlo had cut his hours multiple times over the last few months and had let the majority of his employees go.

It's a shame, she thought. *I would hate to see it close.* The diner had been around for as long as she could remember. She and Candice had often gone there for a burger and fries after school when her daughter was younger, and Candice had even gotten her first job there.

"It's quiet today," he said as she led him over to a small bistro table in the corner. He took off his bowler hat as he sat down, revealing sparse white hair. "You usually have a couple of people in line when I come in for lunch."

"Yeah." She gave a dry laugh. "Thanks to the fact that everyone knows Henry Devou was poisoned by one of my soups, no one wants to eat here anymore."

"I'm sorry about that, Moira. That man is bad for business even when he's dead." Arlo shook his head. "I can't say I was sorry to hear the news though. World's better off without him, if you ask me."

"You don't mean that," she said, shocked. "I know that we've both been seeing fewer profits since his business took off, but he definitely didn't deserve to die."

"It's not just about losing customers to him. That man was wrecking the town. Maple Creek is about tradition and sticking together." He grimaced. "Henry Devou was just another big businessman that didn't care about anything except money. We don't need people like that in our town."

Moira was speechless. She knew that Arlo was old-fashioned, and like many other elderly people, had gotten used to speaking his mind, but this was just too much. It was never okay to talk about the dead like that, at least not in her book.

"I think you should take your soup to go, Arlo," she said. "I need to get back to work."

Even though the conversation with him had ended unpleasantly, it had given Moira a lot to think about.

Maybe she and David were way off target when they had thought that Henry's sister had killed him. Could it be that the diner owner had done it? And if so, why was he trying to frame her? She decided to contact David with her new information; hopefully, they would figure this out soon.

"So, do you really think it could be this Arlo guy?" David asked, his voice tinny over the phone.

"I don't know. The diner is everything to him, though. If it's about to go out of business, he might be feeling desperate. And with what he said about Devou destroying the town... it sounds like he really hated the man." She sighed. She had known Arlo her whole life. Could he really have done it?

"Well, I'll look into it," the detective assured her. "Let me know if you think of anything else."

CHAPTER FIFTEEN

Anticipating another slow day, Moira decided to take advantage of the downtime to experiment. For most of her soups, sandwiches, and salads, she took old favorites and gave them a delicious new twist, but Moira was itching to create something unique. She began by mixing together a few cups of vegetable stock, a couple of tablespoons of soy sauce, and a dash of powdered ginger root in a big pot which she set over a low flame. That would simmer while she chopped the vegetables.

She wanted this to be a colorful soup—she thought she might use it for one of her spring specials— which meant digging the last of the rainbow carrots out of the freezer. She had bought them from an organic hobby farmer at the last farmer's market of the season and had been saving them for something special. They would definitely serve to make the soup unique. Not many people even knew that purple, red, white, and yellow carrots existed, let alone that each color had a different variety of nutrients and a slightly different flavor.

She set the colorful bowl of sliced carrots aside and opened the fridge to figure out what else she wanted to put in her new creation. She had already decided that it would be vegetarian, so she wouldn't be adding any meats. Bok choy was just the thing for this soup, she decided. It would go well with the soy flavoring, and she could create a sandwich that incorporated bok choy leaves, which would tie the two dishes together nicely. *Where is it?* she thought, peering into the refrigerator. *I know we have some.* She had used it in a salad just the other day.

Moira moved some mushrooms aside to look behind them, thinking *I might add some of those too*, and paused. There was a small bag with something green in the very back of the fridge. She always kept fresh herbs in the front since they had to be used quickly or they would lose their flavor. The back of the fridge was only for large items that wouldn't get lost in the shuffle. Plus, all her ingredients were clearly labeled and dated—this bag had neither on it.

She reached in and took the bag out, absently closing the fridge door with her hip as she moved over to the counter to examine the little plant. Was one of her employees doing drugs? She didn't test them, but they all knew that she had a zero tolerance policy.

It wasn't a plant that she recognized off the top of her head, but it looked somewhat familiar. She was an avid gardener in the warmer months, so chances were that she had come across the plant in some gardening book or the other.

She decided to do a quick Internet search before she asked Darrin, who was out front, if he recognized it. The only problem was, what should she search for? It looked almost like the tops of carrots or parsnips, so she decided to start there. Candice had tried to teach her how to use keywords when she was looking things up, but Moira wasn't very confident of her own ability to do it correctly, so she took the easy route. Typing *plants that look like carrots* into the search engine brought her results quickly. She clicked on the first link and began comparing pictures to the plant on the counter in front of her.

A few seconds later, a chill went through her. She looked from the plant to the screen and back again, hoping that she had made a mistake, but there was no doubt. The little green plant that had been hidden at the back of her fridge was hemlock. Now the question was, who had put a deadly plant in her fridge... and why?

CHAPTER SIXTEEN

David stared at his computer screen, tapping a foot on the ground as he tried to draw lines where there just weren't any. Mathilda Devou had just made an appearance on the local news, thanking the public for their support after her brother's death. The only problem was, she had also explained that she was selling the franchise, as she had no interest in running a business. She would be donating all the proceeds to his favorite charity.

Well, he thought, *that takes away any motive she could have had to kill him*. Her tears looked real, and the sadness in her voice was unmistakable. He had to accept that Mathilda Devou was no longer a realistic suspect in the murder case.

Maybe Moira was right, and it was the diner owner. He had never spoken to Arlo himself, but he knew the diner; it was impossible not to drive by it when he was passing through Maple Creek. But just because the old man had motive, it didn't mean that he had done it. It seemed like half the town had a reason to want Henry Devou dead. *The motive may be there, but the evidence just isn't*, he thought.

So, where does that leave Moira? he wondered. He had to admit to himself that with the Devou sister out of the picture, the evidence just kept pointing back to his client. He made a mental list: the bowl of poisoned soup from her deli, her declining business, her lack of alibi for Saturday—although Moira's alibi for Friday was strong, David wished she'd gone out with friends on Saturday... it just didn't look good. She was in the deli almost every day, and wouldn't have had to pay for the soup, which meant there would be no paper trail. And even though she and Henry Devou had been competitors, he would have known her well enough to answer the door if she knocked. From what he had seen of Moira, she was smart enough to trick the man into eating the soup somehow.

There were two things that didn't make sense to him. If Moira had committed the crime, why had she left so much evidence behind? She must have known that the police would be able to track the to-go bowl back to her; it had her deli's logo on it, after all. And if his client was guilty, then why had she hired him?

He knew that his little business had a good reputation; he wasn't some hack investigator trying to make an easy buck. No, he was a professional, and his track record showed it. He also knew that his services didn't come cheaply. Why would she pay to have someone prove that she was guilty?

Maybe he was over-thinking things. His first mentor had always told him that the simplest explanation was usually the right one. Chances were, there wasn't some big conspiracy to make Moira look guilty. If he were to think about this case logically, then the answer was obvious; the deli owner was the murderer. But for some reason, his gut still told him that she was innocent. *If Moira didn't poison the soup, then who did?* Suddenly the answer was right in front of him, so obvious that he didn't understand how he hadn't seen it before. Someone at the deli *had* killed Henry Devou, but it wasn't Moira. There was someone else that had a motive to kill Henry, someone that he had overlooked so far. Someone that Moira trusted and confided in... someone that had been doing their hardest to pin the crime on someone else. David grabbed his overcoat and keys and rushed out of his office.

CHAPTER SEVENTEEN

Moira carefully wrapped the deadly little plant back up in the bag and slipped it into her pocket. Her new soup could wait; right now, she had to find a murderer and clear her name.

"Darrin, something came up. Can you handle the store on your own until Danielle gets here?" she asked as she strode out of the kitchen.

"Sure, Ms. D., not a problem, it's not like we're busy right now." He looked at her with concern on his face. "Is everything alright?"

"Not yet, but it will be," she said grimly. "You just hold tight. I'll explain everything later."

Moira got into her car before taking out her cell phone and dialing David Morris's number. She tapped the steering wheel impatiently as it rang. When the call went to voicemail, she left a quick message asking him to call her back and then hung up, frustrated. She wanted to tell the private detective about her find and ask him what she should do next. Going straight to the police probably wouldn't be a good idea; there was no way that they would believe the story about her just happening to find the hemlock in her fridge.

Putting the car into gear, Moira drove out of the parking lot and turned down the road that would take her to Lake Marion. She would keep trying to get David on his phone while she drove, and if it came to it, she would try to find him in person at his office. Maybe she should have taken Candice's initial advice and gotten herself a lawyer; someone was definitely trying to frame her for murder, and she was beginning to feel out of her depth.

After a few more calls to David's phone had gone to voicemail, Moira groaned in annoyance and put her phone down. Where had the detective gotten to? She needed him now more than ever, but he was proving impossible to get in touch with.

You don't need him, she told herself. *You're a smart woman. Figure it out yourself.* Well, what did she know so far? Someone had bought a bowl of soup from her store, poisoned it, then had given it to her business competitor. Then someone, presumably the same person, had planted hemlock in her refrigerator at the deli. Moira figured it was safe to assume that Henry Devou had died from hemlock poisoning, even though there was no way for her to confirm that now.

So, whoever had murdered Henry had also managed to get into her kitchen somehow, without her or any of her employees noticing. How was that possible? Most nights, she herself was the one to lock the building up, and she always double-checked the doors before going home. If she had somehow forgotten a door, or someone had picked the lock, then her employees would surely have mentioned finding an unlocked door the next morning.

It was unlikely that anyone had snuck into the kitchen during the day. There were usually at least two employees on staff: one up front to take orders and pack up the refrigerated items for customers, and the other employee in the back to keep an eye on the soup, to slice bread and cold cuts, and just to keep things flowing smoothly. If a customer had been found in the kitchen, she would definitely have been told.

So, what was the answer? Moira gripped the steering wheel harder, frustrated by the whole situation. It looked like she was dealing with a professional, someone who could pick locks and was smart enough to re-lock the door behind them when they left probably wasn't an amateur at this kind of thing. Was David right? Had Henry's sister done the whole thing? When she had confronted Moira, she had seemed genuinely upset. And from what she had seen of Henry's sister, she wasn't exactly the subtle type.

The big question was how this person managed to be so invisible. She and David had gone over the likely possibilities together, and she had asked each of her employees if they remembered seeing any of those people in the few days before Henry Devou had been murdered. Not a single one had been recognized by Darrin, Danielle, or Candice. It was like someone invisible had bought the soup and planted the hemlock in the fridge.

No, it's not someone invisible, she chided herself. She had to quit avoiding what was staring her in her face. Whoever had killed Henry Devou was someone that knew her well. Someone that had access to the deli and that wouldn't raise suspicion if they were poking around in the kitchen. The terrible realization unfolded slowly inside of her. The murderer was one of her employees.

She tried David's phone once more, with no answer. She couldn't wait to talk to him; she had to act now. It wouldn't be right for her not to tell the police what she knew. What if the murderer was escaping right now? If they checked the fridge and saw that the hemlock was gone, then they would know that she had found out.

As she turned her car around and began making her way back to Maple Creek, there was only one question in her mind. Which one of the people that she worked with had killed Henry Devou?

CHAPTER EIGHTEEN

She didn't want to think that it could be true, even for an instant, but once the thought was in her head, she just couldn't make it go away. Part of her was horrified that she was even considering the fact that one of her employees could be a killer—they were her family, all of them—but another part kept going over the evidence in her mind. The police believed that the poisoned soup had come from the deli because it *had* come from the deli. The poison might even have been added while it was still in the kitchen. All the evidence that they had found so far pointed back to the store that she owned because that's where the murderer had committed the crime.

Moira couldn't believe that she was even entertaining this line of thought. As she had told David, she trusted each of her employees completely. But what if she had been wrong to do so? Everyone had poor judgment sometimes; had she made a fatal mistake when hiring Darrin or Danielle? It couldn't be Candice; she couldn't even consider the idea that her own daughter could kill someone. Besides, Candice would have had no motive. Her daughter was involved with running the business and had seen their finances. She knew that the business was doing well. No, her daughter was not a murderer.

Not knowing exactly what she was going to say, but knowing that she had to get to the bottom of this, Moira pulled into her driveway. She was going to go to the police, but first, she wanted to talk to her daughter. It looked like she would be needing that lawyer after all.

It wasn't until he was more than halfway to Maple Creek that David realized that in his rush to get out the door, he had left his cell phone behind. He huffed out a breath of air in annoyance. Hopefully, he would be able to catch Moira at the deli; she seemed to work constantly anyway, so chances were good that she was there.

When he pulled into the small parking lot outside of Darling's DELIcious Delights, he immediately noticed that her car wasn't there. *Should I look for her at her house?* he wondered. Then he remembered that the only place he had her address was on his cell phone.

Cursing how dependent he was on modern technology and deeply missing his old notepad, David slammed his car door shut and entered the store. Darrin, Moira's young male employee, was at the counter chatting with Danielle.

"Hi, Mr. Morris," he said brightly. "I'm glad you stopped by. This place is dead today. I should have taken Ms. D.'s advice and brought a book with me." Danielle just nodded at him, her face expressionless.

"Is Moira here?" David asked, skipping the pleasantries. He glanced at the two employees, trying not to let his thoughts show on his face. If he was right, then one of them was a killer.

"Well no, she left about an hour ago." Frowning, he asked, "Is something wrong?"

"I don't know," the detective replied truthfully. "Do you know where she went?"

"No, but she didn't look happy. She sort of rushed out of here. Is it about the case, do you think?" the young man asked.

"I'm not sure," David replied, already partway through the front door. "But if you see her, tell her that I'll meet her at the police station."

CHAPTER NINETEEN

The house was empty when Moira got there, and
she groaned in annoyance. She wanted to go to the
police as quickly as possible with her new evidence,
but she didn't want to put herself into their hands
without talking to her daughter first. If the detectives
at the police station didn't believe her, they might
end up arresting her, in which case she would
desperately need her daughter's help.

"Where are you?" she asked when Candice answered
her call.

"I went to the mall. What's up? You sound worried."
The mall was a good forty-five minutes away. Could

PATTI BENNING

she wait that long to go to the police? She would
have to. She didn't want to worry her daughter right
before a long drive on snowy roads.

"I just need to talk to you. It's not an emergency, but
can you head back?" she asked.

"Alright, just let me pay for my clothes, and I'll be on
my way." Candice paused. "Is everything
okay, Mom?"

"I think I made a break in the case," her mother
replied honestly. "And I need to talk to you about it."

Just then, there was a knock at her door. Moira said
goodbye to her daughter and then walked to the
foyer. She unlocked the deadbolt and let the door
swing open, her mind on what she was going to tell
her daughter when she saw her.

Her breath caught in her throat when she saw Danielle standing on her porch. Her normally cheerful employee had a tear-streaked face and eyes red from crying. Moira was about to comfort her when she looked down and saw the gun in her employee's hand.

"Danielle? What are you doing?" she asked, automatically taking a step backward.

"I'm so sorry, Ms. D., I don't want to go to jail." The young woman choked back a sob. "I thought that they would just arrest you and it would all be over, but you kept making things worse."

"It was you. You killed him." Moira backed up further, putting her hands up as she'd seen people do on TV. The entrance to the kitchen was right behind her. What could she do in there? Grab a knife?

"I just don't understand... why?" she asked, trying to bide for time while coming up with a plan. "Why would you throw your future away? Why would you *kill* someone?" Moira's voice broke on the last sentence. She had never felt such hurt and betrayal, not even when her ex-husband had filed for divorce.

"What future?" The girl gave a short, harsh laugh. "I should have been the rich and famous one, not him. It should be *me* in all the town papers, me who opened stores across the state. He took away my chance at success, so I took away his."

"I don't understand."

"All those soups that made the Soup Shoppe so famous? They were my recipes, Ms. D., I did all the hard work, I poured my *soul* into cooking, and he claimed it all for himself," her face twisted with anger and she continued, "every single time someone mentioned his restaurant, or his franchise, or how good his food was, they should have been saying *my* restaurant, *my* food."

"He claimed all the credit for the things that you did? I'm sorry, sweetie." And she was. She knew how much went in to creating a new recipe, and how wonderful it felt when someone enjoyed it. But that came nowhere near excusing Danielle's crime. Not in the eyes of the law, and definitely not to Moira. "I don't understand; why didn't you just tell someone?"

"Who would believe me?" the young woman asked in a defeated voice. "I was just some kid that was good with soups. He was the rich businessman with a team of lawyers. When I finally got fed up with it and told him I was going to stop coming up with new soups for him, he fired me."

"So, you came up with a plan to kill him." The level of hatred and resentment that had gone into this murder astounded Moira. Danielle had always seemed so sweet and quiet. "But why did you try to pin it on me?" She had kept backing up slowly and now felt the back of her legs press into the kitchen cabinet. She didn't dare look behind her for a knife or, better yet, her phone. Was there anything here that could save her? Her gaze drifted past Danielle's shoulder to where her front door was still standing open. If only she could make it past her employee, she might be able to escape.

"I didn't, at first. But once the police started being all suspicious of you, I thought that it would be an easy way to get them off of my trail. All I really did was leave the extra hemlock in the fridge so that if they got a search warrant, they would find evidence that would tie you to the crime, and I also told Detective Fitzgerald that you'd said the Soup Shoppe was running us out of business." She shrugged. "I didn't really have to do much. I felt bad about it I guess, but I just... I can't go to jail."

"And the soup? How did you get him to eat it?" Moira managed to ask, keeping her eyes on the gun which was pointed at her stomach now.

"I just told him that I wanted my job back and that the soup was a sample of a new recipe I had just come up with. He was so greedy, he didn't even question it."

"Do you feel better, now that he's gone?" the older woman asked quietly.

"I did at first," she admitted. "But then the investigation started, and I wished that I could take it back. Or at least do it smarter. It's all that stupid investigator's fault. He's the only one that doesn't think it's you."

"David is far from stupid, I wouldn't underestimate him." Moira leaned against the edge of the counter and closed her eyes, emotionally exhausted. "Please, Danielle, just put the gun down. We can figure this out. Killing me won't help things."

"I think I can make it look like you killed yourself,"

her employee said. "And I'll write a note on your computer saying you did it and felt guilty. It's the only way I can save myself, Ms. D., I'm sorry." Moira opened her eyes to see the barrel of the gun pointed at her face. Her heart pounding, she watched as the desperate young woman clicked off the safety.

"You can close your eyes again, if you want," Danielle said, using one of her hands to wipe tears from her eyes. "It might make it easier."

For you or for me? Moira wondered. She was opening her mouth to talk more—to say something, anything, to stall–but her mind was blank. Was this really it? Was this how she would die? *Oh, my goodness*, she thought. *Candice will be home soon. She'll be the one to find my body.*

The sound of a car pulling into her driveway made Danielle pause. Moira had no idea who it could be; it was way too early for her daughter to have made it home, and no one else would come over without calling first. Suddenly she realized that this was her chance; Danielle was looking back over her shoulder, and the gun was wavering.

Reaching behind her, she hoped to find something that she could use to defend herself. She tried not to move too much, so that she didn't draw the girl's gaze back, but her hand only found empty counter.

Then her fingers brushed something. A paper bag filled with something. She had no idea what it was, but it would have to do because Danielle was turning her head back towards her.

"What are you..." she began, just moments before Moira swung the paper bag towards her and a cloud of flour filled the air.

Moira dived to the side, and just in time—an earsplitting bang sounded, and chips of wood flew from the cabinets behind where she had been standing. The flour was already settling, leaving Danielle and half of Moira's kitchen covered in the fine powder.

The gun, Moira thought. The young woman seemed to have forgotten it as she tried to rub the flour out of her eyes, but she knew Danielle's distraction wouldn't last for long. She lunged for the weapon, her fingers closing over Danielle's. She tried to tug it away, but the girl wasn't giving up without a fight. They struggled back and forth for a few seconds, and somehow a second shot went off, missing Moira's foot by an inch.

"Freeze!" The command was shouted from the doorway to her kitchen, surprising both women badly enough that they stopped moving. She looked over to see the tall, imposing private investigator standing just feet away, his gun out and pointed at Danielle. Moira recovered from the shock first and wrested her employee's firearm out of her grip.

David glanced up at her, relieved. "Are you okay? She didn't shoot you?"

"No, I'm... well, I'm not hurt." She had been about to say that she was fine, but that would be a lie. She felt like she would never be fine again. "Are you okay?"

"Yes... hold on..." He reached into his pocket and tossed a pair of handcuffs to her. Nodding at Danielle, he said, "You know what to do."

Shaking all over, Moira gingerly put the gun down on the counter, well out of reach, before approaching the flour-covered young woman who was standing in front of her. Danielle didn't resist as she put the handcuffs on her, and even after everything Moira couldn't help feeling bad for her.

"I'm glad you're alright," David said softly when she was done. "When I saw her car in your driveway, I knew that you had figured it out too."

"I did, just in time. What now?" she asked, feeling numb as she looked at her former employee in cuffs before her.

"Now, we call the police," he said. "I'm sure they'll be glad to know that we found their murderer."

CHAPTER TWENTY

When Moira saw the detective come through the
front door of her deli, she excused herself and asked
Darrin to take care of the customer that she had
been speaking to. Business was back to normal—
better than normal, in fact. It seemed like everyone
in town wanted to talk to the woman who had been
held at gunpoint by a killer.

"It's good to see this place alive again," David said
when she approached him. "I'm glad things are
looking up for you."

"I am too. I just wish that it hadn't come at such a

price." She didn't know if she would ever be able to recover from the shock of finding out that one of her employees had killed someone. It would be hard to trust someone new after this, but with the extra business from all the publicity that the news had been giving them, and with tourist season looming only a few months away, she would have to hire someone else soon.

"You never really know people as well as you think you do," he said softly.

"Are you still planning on moving?" asked Moira. She found herself hoping that the handsome detective would stay around.

"Those plans are on hold for now." He grinned and sat next to her. "I've been picking up new clients left and right; it looks like all I needed was some TV face time to inspire people to hire me to solve the mysteries in their lives."

"I guess they realized that terrible things can happen even in small towns, and they want someone like you on their side." She smiled at him. "Thanks for supporting me and helping me figure out the truth, no matter how terrible it was."

"It's all in my job description," he said.

"Saving me from being shot isn't," Moira said, her tone soft but serious. "So, thank you."

"It was my pleasure," he responded. Neither of them said anything for a moment, and then David cleared his throat. "Well, I should get going. I just wanted to stop in and see how things were. You know where to find me if you manage to get into trouble again." He shook her hand once more and then disappeared through the front door. Moira watched him go, feeling a twinge of loneliness for a moment. Then Darrin called her name, Candice walked out of the kitchen with a tray of cold cuts balanced on one hand, and Moira felt herself smile again. She had a lot to be thankful for and a lot to look forward to. Life might not always be easy, but with the people she trusted by her side, she could take it one step at a time.

Papa Pacelli's Series

Book 1: Pall Bearers and Pepperoni

Book 2: Bacon Cheddar Murder

Book 3: Very Veggie Murder

Book 4: Italian Wedding Murder

Book 5: Smoked Gouda Murder

Book 6: Gourmet Holiday Murder

Book 7: Four Cheese Murder

Book 8: Hand Tossed Murder

Book 9: Exotic Pizza Murder

Book 10: Fiesta Pizza Murder

Book 11: Garlic Artichoke Murder

Book 12: On the Wings of Murder

Book 13: Mozzarella and Murder

Book 14: A Thin Crust of Murder

Book 15: Pretzel Pizza Murder

Book 16: Parmesan Pizza Murder

Book 17: Breakfast Pizza Murder

Book 18: Halloween Pizza Murder

Book 19: Thanksgiving Pizza Murder

Book 20: Christmas Pizza Murder

Book 21: A Crispy Slice of Murder

Book 22: Lobster Pizza Murder

Book 23: Pizza, Weddings, and Murder

Book 24: Pizza, Paradise, and Murder

Book 25: Meat Lovers and Murder

Book 26: Classic Crust Murder

Book 27: Hot, Spicy Murder

Book 28: Pork, Pizza, and Murder

Book 29: Chicken Alfredo Murder

Book 30: Jalapeño Pizza Murder

Book 31: Pesto Pizza Murder

Book 32: Sweet Chili Murder

Book 33: A Melted Morsel of Murder

Book34: A Saucy Taste of Murder

Book 35: A Crunchy Crust of Murder

Book 36: Shrimply Sublime Murder

Book 37: Boldly Basil Murder

Darling Deli Series

Book 1: Pastrami Murder

Book 2: Corned Beef Murder

Book 3: Cold Cut Murder

Book 4: Grilled Cheese Murder

Book 5: Chicken Pesto Murder

Book 6: Thai Coconut Murder

Book 7: Tomato Basil Murder

Book 8: Salami Murder

Book 9: Hearty Homestyle Murder

Book 10: Honey BBQ Murder

Book 11: Beef Brisket Murder

Book 12: Garden Vegetable Murder

Book 13: Spicy Lasagna Murder

Book 14: Curried Lobster Murder

Book 15: Creamy Casserole Murder

Book 16: Grilled Rye Murder

Book 17: A Quiche to Die For

Book 18: A Side of Murder

Book 19: Wrapped in Murder

Book 20: Glazed Ham Murder

Book 21: Chicken Club Murder

Book 22: Pies, Lies and Murder

Book 23: Mountains, Marriage and Murder

Book 24: Shrimply Murder

Book 25: Gazpacho Murder

Book 26: Peppered with Murder

Book 27: Ravioli Soup Murder

Book 28: Thanksgiving Deli Murder

Book 29: A Season of Murder

Book 30: Valentines and Murder

Book 31: Shamrocks and Murder

Book 32: Sugar Coated Murder

Book 33: Murder, My Darling

Killer Cookie Series

Book 1: Killer Caramel Cookies

Book 2: Killer Halloween Cookies

Book 3: Killer Maple Cookies

Book 4: Crunchy Christmas Murder

Book 5: Killer Valentine Cookies

Asheville Meadows Series

Book 1: Small Town Murder

Book 2: Murder on Aisle Three

Book 3: The Heart of Murder

Book 4: Dating is Murder

Book 5: Dying to Cook

Book 6: Food, Family and Murder

Book 7: Fish, Chips and Murder

Cozy Mystery Tails of Alaska

Book 1: Mushing is Murder

Book 2: Murder Befalls Us

Book 3: Stage Fright and Murder

Book 4: Routine Murder

Book 5: Best Friends and Betrayal

Book 6: Tick Tock and Treachery

AUTHOR'S NOTE

I'd love to hear your thoughts on my books, the storylines, and anything else that you'd like to comment on—reader feedback is very important to me. My contact information, along with some other helpful links, is listed on the next page. If you'd like to be on my list of "folks to contact" with updates, release and sales notifications, etc.... just shoot me an email and let me know. Thanks for reading!

Also...

... if you're looking for more great reads, Summer Prescott Books publishes several popular series by outstanding Cozy Mystery authors.

CONTACT SUMMER PRESCOTT
BOOKS PUBLISHING

Twitter: @summerprescott1

Bookbub:
https://www.bookbub.com/authors/summer-prescott

Blog and Book Catalog:
http://summerprescottbooks.com

Email: summer.prescott.cozies@gmail.com

YouTube:
https://www.youtube.com/channel/UCngKNUkDd
WuQ5k7-Vkfrp6A

And...be sure to check out the Summer Prescott Cozy Mysteries fan page and Summer Prescott Books Publishing Page on Facebook – let's be friends!

To download a free book, and sign up for our fun and exciting newsletter, which will give you opportunities to win prizes and swag, enter contests, and be the first to know about New Releases, click here: http://summerprescottbooks.com

Made in the USA
Coppell, TX
01 March 2021